From up on the carousel horse Timothy could see out the high window. "What was that?" he said suddenly.

"What was what?" asked Titus and Sarah-Jane.

"I thought I saw someone looking in!" Timothy answered. But when he looked again, the face was gone.

"This is a case for the T.C.D.C."

THE MYSTERY OF THE

CAROUSEL
HORSE

Elspeth Campbell Murphy
Illustrated by Chris Wold Dyrud

Chariot Books
David C. Cook Publishing Co.

A Wise Owl Book
Published by Chariot Books,
an imprint of David C. Cook Publishing Co.
David C. Cook Publishing Co., Elgin, Illinois 60120
David C. Cook Publishing Co., Weston, Ontario

The Mystery of the Carousel Horse
© 1988 by Elspeth Campbell Murphy for text and Chris Wold
Dyrud for illustrations

Cover design by Chris Patchel
First Printing, 1988
Printed in the United States of America

98 97 96 95   10 9 8

Library of Congress Cataloging-in-Publication Data
Murphy, Elspeth Campbell.
  The mystery of the carousel horse.

  (The Ten commandments mysteries)
  Summary: The efforts of three cousins to keep an elderly
neighbor from being cheated out of an antique wooden carousel
horse help them understand the Biblical commandment, "You shall
not covet."
  [1. Greed—Fiction. 2. Cousins—Fiction. 3. Ten
commandments—Fiction. 4. Mystery and detective stories.]
I. Dyrud, Chris Wold, ill. II. Title. III. Series:
Murphy, Elspeth Campbell. Ten Commandments mysteries.
PZ7.M95316Mx   1988   [FIC]   87-16722
ISBN 1-55513-163-8

''You shall not covet.''

Exodus 20:17 (NIV)

The author wishes to thank Tobin Fraley of Tobin Fraley Studios for his most valuable information on antique carousel horses. Mr. Fraley is the author of *The Carousel Animal*, Zephyr Press.

CONTENTS

1
MORE DETECTIVE WORK?

The three cousins, Timothy Dawson, Titus Mc-Kay, and Sarah-Jane Cooper, sat on Sarah-Jane's front porch and wondered how to spend the day.

The morning was hot and still. The cousins hadn't even had breakfast yet, but already they were feeling bored and almost crabby.

"What do *you* guys want to do?" asked Titus, who was visiting from the city.

"I don't know," said Timothy, who was visiting from the suburbs. "What do *you* guys want to do?"

"I don't know," said Sarah-Jane, who lived in the sleepy old town of Fairfield. "What do *you* guys want to do?"

Timothy and Titus just shrugged.

Sarah-Jane said dreamily, "I wish something

exciting and fun would happen. I wish we had another mystery to solve."

Just as she said that, the cousins saw Sarah-Jane's friend and neighbor, old Miss Amelia Featherstone, coming briskly along the sidewalk toward Sarah-Jane's house, carrying clipboards.

Miss Featherstone went to the same church as the Coopers. Sarah-Jane's mother always said, "I don't know what this church would do without Miss Featherstone. She's the most *organized* person I know!"

She was also one of the *nicest* people anyone knew. So maybe that's why people from the church and the town were always coming to her when they needed help.

Of course, sometimes Miss Featherstone needed help herself. In fact, just a few days ago, the cousins had helped her by solving a hundred-year-old mystery.

Miss Featherstone called, "Good morning, Timothy, Titus, and Sarah-Jane! I have a job for you, if you're interested."

The cousins scrambled down the steps and ran to meet her.

10

"More detective work?" asked Sarah-Jane eagerly.

"Well, no, not exactly," said Miss Featherstone. "But I'll pay each person fifty cents an hour. And it's the kind of work that needs good detectives—people who are smart and thorough and who notice things. That's why I came to you."

"Great!" cried Timothy. "What's the job?"

"Helping Mrs. Bradley take inventory," said Miss Featherstone.

"What does 'taking inventory' mean?" asked

Titus.

Miss Featherstone explained. "We're going to look over lots and lots of stuff and make a note of what's there. You'll have to be observant, so it's good *practice* detective work."

"Do we get to write on those clipboards?" asked Sarah-Jane.

"Oh, yes, indeed," said Miss Featherstone. And she handed them each a clipboard filled with smooth white sheets of lined paper. Attached to each clipboard by a long string was a freshly sharpened pencil. And on top of each pencil was a brand-new eraser cap.

Miss Featherstone said, "I'd be so glad if you can help! It will make Mrs. Bradley's garage sale go a lot easier!"

The cousins looked at one another doubtfully. *A garage sale?* That didn't sound very exciting. And not the least bit mysterious.

Miss Featherstone laughed as if she knew what they were thinking. "Have you eaten yet? If not, I'll take you out to breakfast and tell you all about this job. Believe me, Mrs. Bradley really needs us! She's had a hard time lately. By helping with the garage sale, we can show her that the church really cares about her.''

''Then count me in,'' said Timothy.

''Me, too,'' said Titus.

''I'll tell my mom,'' said Sarah-Jane.

She was back in a minute, and the four of them set off for the Copper Kettle coffee shop on Main Street.

2

THE FAIRFIELD CAROUSEL

The Copper Kettle coffee shop was across the street from the library.

The library was celebrating its 100th anniversary, so it had a lot of old-time photographs of Fairfield on display.

Miss Featherstone and the cousins stopped to look at the pictures before going over for breakfast.

The library had just opened for the day, so they had the pictures almost all to themselves. Two men were already there. They were studying the pictures and talking quietly but excitedly.

Timothy, Titus, and Sarah-Jane started asking Miss Featherstone all kinds of questions about the old days. Miss Featherstone had lived in Fairfield all her life, so she knew a lot about these

photographs.

Suddenly Sarah-Jane squealed, "Ooo! Look at this picture of the merry-go-round!"

The two men turned and stared at her for a moment. Then they quickly looked away.

Sarah-Jane remembered that she was in a library and spoke more softly. "That looks like the park by the river," she said to Miss Featherstone. "But I never saw a merry-go-round there!"

"No," said Miss Featherstone sadly. "It's long gone. But, oh! What a lovely carousel it was! Beautiful wooden horses. All hand carved.

15

Each one different from the others. They don't make them like that anymore." She laughed. "I guess old people say that about a lot of things."

Timothy asked, "How do they make merry-go-rounds now?"

"By machine, I would imagine," said Miss Featherstone. "And they're probably made out of metal or fiberglass instead of wood."

"Did you used to ride the old wooden merry-go-round?" asked Sarah-Jane.

Miss Featherstone nodded. "Oh, yes! My goodness, this old photograph brings back memories! People used to come down to the river park for a picnic lunch. And we children would ride round and round on the carousel. We'd pretend to be knights or cowboys or princesses."

Titus said, "But why isn't the carousel there anymore?"

Miss Featherstone smiled gently. "The Great Depression hit, Titus, and just about everyone was poor. No one could afford treats like merry-go-round rides anymore. I think the family who owned the carousel took it apart. They probably sold the horses to bigger amusement parks. But soon even the bigger parks went out of business. Come to think of it, I believe it was Mr. Bradley's family who owned the Fairfield carousel. And I was going to tell you about Mrs. Bradley's garage sale.''

"Over breakfast,'' said Timothy.

"I'm hungry!'' said Titus.

"Then enough of old photographs!'' said Miss Featherstone with a laugh. "Look out, Copper Kettle! Here we come!''

Miss Featherstone and the cousins left the library and went across the street to the coffee shop.

A couple of minutes later, the two men from the library came in and sat in the booth right behind them.

3

BREAKFAST AT THE COPPER KETTLE

Over pancakes and sausages Miss Featherstone explained why Mrs. Bradley needed their help.

"Mr. Bradley died not too long ago," she said. "He had been sick for a long time. Now Mrs. Bradley has huge hospital bills to pay. And she doesn't have the money she needs. So she's thinking she'll have to sell her house. But she'll have to clear out *a lot* of stuff first! You see, Mr. Bradley never threw *anything* away!"

Sarah-Jane said, "Maybe people will buy the stuff Mr. Bradley saved. If Mrs. Bradley has a garage sale, she could get rid of stuff—and make some money at the same time."

"That's the idea exactly," agreed Miss Featherstone. "The sale won't bring nearly *enough* money, of course, but every little bit helps. And our first step is to see what there is to sell.''

Timothy wiped away his milk moustache with a napkin. "Hmmm," he said. "Who knows *what* we'll find?''

Sarah-Jane and Miss Featherstone made some guesses. But Titus didn't say anything. In fact, he hadn't said a word all during breakfast.

While Miss Featherstone stopped to talk to a friend, Timothy, Titus, and Sarah-Jane stepped out into the hot sunshine. It actually felt kind of nice after the chilly, air-conditioned restaurant.

Sarah-Jane waved to Mr. Robinson, who was unlocking his antique store.

Titus said, "Tim. S-J. Let me ask you something. Did you ever get the feeling someone was listening to everything you said?''

"Like when they're not supposed to?" asked Sarah-Jane. "You mean, eavesdropping?''

"Who was doing that?" asked Timothy.

Titus whispered, "Don't look now. But you see those two men who were in the library? They're in line to pay.''

Timothy and Sarah-Jane looked, but they made

it seem like they weren't looking at anything in particular.

"What about them?" asked Timothy.

"Shh!" said Titus. Suddenly he knelt down and pretended to find a really interesting rock. Timothy and Sarah-Jane didn't ask questions. They just stooped down beside him.

The restaurant door opened, and the two men came out. The men walked right past the cousins without noticing them.

Titus quickly looked around to make sure the coast was clear. "I was sitting right behind those guys at breakfast. And they didn't say *a thing* to each other the whole time. I think that's because they were listening to *us*. You know how you can just tell that sometimes? And I think they were listening to us back in the library, too."

Timothy said, "But why would they eavesdrop on us? What were we talking about that was so interesting?"

Sarah-Jane frowned thoughtfully, trying to remember. She said, "Part of the time in the library the men were talking to each other about the old-time pictures. Then maybe they listened in to us

because they wanted to hear Miss Featherstone tell about the old days. But at breakfast we weren't talking about anything special. Just garage sales. Why would they want to hear about Mrs. Bradley's garage sale?''

Timothy said, ''People get weird about garage sales. We had one at my house once. It was supposed to start at nine o'clock. But some people came and knocked on our door at *six-thirty in the morning*! So maybe these guys just wanted to find out about Mrs. Bradley's sale, so they can get there first.''

Titus and Sarah-Jane agreed that Timothy was probably right. But the three of them also agreed that it was all still mysterious. They were even more sure of that when they were walking with Miss Featherstone to Mrs. Bradley's house. A car drove slowly past them. And in the car were the same two men.

4
A HORSE'S HOOF?

Mrs. Bradley came out to meet Timothy, Titus, and Sarah-Jane.

"Hello, Lenora!" called Miss Featherstone cheerfully. "Never fear—the T.C.D.C. is here!"

Mrs. Bradley smiled at the cousins, but she looked a little puzzled. "What's a 'teesy-deesy'?" she asked.

"It's letters," explained Timothy and Titus together.

"Capital T.

Capital C.

Capital D.

Capital C.

It stands for the Three Cousins Detective Club."

Sarah-Jane said, "Our favorite job is solving mysteries. But Miss Featherstone said good detectives have to notice things. So we're going to notice what you can sell at your garage sale."

"Well, actually," said Mrs. Bradley as she led them around behind the house, "it's more like a *barn* sale."

And sure enough—there, at the end of the long yard, was a small barn.

Now it was the cousins' turn to be puzzled.

"Do you keep *animals* in there?" asked Timothy.

Mrs. Bradley sighed. "Maybe when my husband was a little boy his family had a few farm animals," she said. "But over the years it has just gotten filled—WITH JUNK!"

"Now, Lenora, don't be discouraged," said Miss Featherstone. "I'm sure it's not *all* junk. It's like Timothy said at breakfast, 'Who knows *what* we'll find?' "

Mrs. Bradley threw open the barn doors, and the five of them stepped inside.

There was so much stuff, Mrs. Bradley and the cousins wanted to give up right then and there. But Miss Featherstone—who was very organized—wouldn't let them.

24

So Mrs. Bradley opened the windows and switched on the lights.

Miss Featherstone assigned each of the cousins to a different part of the barn. She told them to write down what they saw.

"And I want your advice, too," Miss Featherstone added. "Beside each item on the list, mark whether you think Mrs. Bradley should keep it or sell it or throw it away."

So Timothy, Titus, and Sarah-Jane split up and got right to work. They wrote down lamps and picture frames, bottles and tennis rackets, and on and on.

Sarah-Jane was feeling hot and dusty and worn out, when she came to something big in her corner. It was covered with canvas dust sheets.

Sarah-Jane lifted the corner and peeked underneath. *A horse's hoof???*

Quickly Sarah-Jane pulled off the dust sheets. Then she jumped back with a gasp.

She was looking at the most beautiful thing she had ever seen in her life.

"Tim! Ti! Come here quick!"

The boys hurried over, stepping across rakes

and rocking chairs and newspapers.

"Wow!" breathed Timothy when he saw it. "Neat-O!"

"EXcellent!" whispered Titus.

Quickly Sarah-Jane wrote down on her list: *One beautiful merry-go-round horse—KEEP KEEP KEEP.*

5
A FACE AT THE WINDOW

Miss Featherstone and Mrs. Bradley came over to see what all the excitement was about.

"Tom's old carousel horse!" exclaimed Mrs. Bradley. "It's belonged to our family for years. I had almost forgotten about it."

"Lenora!" said Miss Featherstone in amazement. "Do you mean to tell us that this horse was once part of the Fairfield carousel?"

Mrs. Bradley nodded. "Did you know that Tom's family owned the carousel? Well, when they lost the business, Tom's father let him keep his favorite horse. They set it up here in the barn, so that Tom could 'ride' it whenever he wanted."

Of course, Timothy, Titus, and Sarah-Jane were just *dying* to sit on the horse!

Mrs. Bradley checked to make sure it was still

safe. Then the cousins took turns climbing on.

"Oh, Mrs. Bradley!" cried Sarah-Jane. "You have to keep this beautiful horse forever and ever!"

But Mrs. Bradley just smiled and shook her head. "I'm afraid I can't, Honey. I'll be moving to a smaller place. And I won't have room to store it."

"So you mean you're going to *sell* it?" asked Timothy.

Mrs. Bradley turned to Miss Featherstone. "What do you think, Amelia? Is this the kind of thing someone would buy?"

"It's in excellent condition," said Miss Featherstone. "Maybe someone with lots of room will buy it for a decoration."

Mrs. Bradley turned back to the cousins with a smile. "Tell you what," she said. "If I can sell the horse, I will, because I really need the money. But if no one wants to buy it, I will give it to Sarah-Jane, and she can share it with Timothy and Titus when they come to visit."

"Neat-O!" cried Timothy.

"EXcellent!" cheered Titus.

"Oh, I hope, hope, *hope* we can have it!" said Sarah-Jane.

It was time to break for lunch. Mrs. Bradley went to make hot dogs, and the cousins played some more on the horse.

It was Timothy's turn again. From up on the horse he could see out the high window. "What was that?" he said suddenly.

"What was what?" asked Titus and Sarah-Jane.

"I thought I saw someone looking in!" said Timothy.

But when he looked again, the face was gone.

And when they checked outside, there was no one there.

All they heard was Mrs. Bradley calling them to lunch—and a car driving away up the alley.

Sarah-Jane called home to let her mother know they were staying for lunch. But she had to use the neighbor's phone, because Mrs. Bradley's phone was out of order.

"The repairman is supposed to come this afternoon," said Mrs. Bradley. She and Miss Featherstone decided to make the garage sale signs out on the front porch, so they wouldn't miss him. Besides, it was too hot to do any more work in the barn.

Timothy, Titus, and Sarah-Jane promised to come back the next morning. Miss Featherstone said they could take their clipboards with them, as long as they remembered to bring them back.

Then each cousin got a dollar for two hours of taking inventory.

"And a bonus," said Mrs. Bradley, giving them each another fifty cents. "I didn't have anything for dessert, so maybe you can go to Dairy-Delite."

"Great idea! Thanks!" said the cousins.

They waved good-bye to Mrs. Bradley and Miss Featherstone and headed for the ice-cream stand on Main Street.

There was a long line at the Dairy-Delite window. The cousins got at the end of it. But suddenly they noticed the two men again. They were leaving the window and carrying sundaes to one of the little outside tables.

"Now it's *our* turn to eavesdrop!" whispered Titus.

Quickly and quietly the cousins slipped out of line and scooted around the building to the other side where the tables were. They scrunched down behind a large garbage can.

"It's incredible!" they heard the first man say. "That old lady is sitting on a gold mine, and she doesn't even know it!"

"And she's not going to find out!" said the second man. "I'm going to get my hands on that

treasure if it's the last thing I do!''

"We have to act fast," said the first man.

"Yeah," said the second. "But we've got to look casual. We don't want her to get suspicious."

The cousins stayed in hiding until they saw the men drive off.

7

AN EXPERT OPINION

"I *knew* it!" exclaimed Timothy. "They were *spying* on us at Mrs. Bradley's!"

Titus said, "What did they mean about 'gold mine' and 'treasure'? I didn't see any gold or jewels in the barn. Did you guys?"

Timothy and Sarah-Jane shook their heads.

Titus went on, "But maybe they didn't *exactly* mean gold. Maybe they just meant the treasure was something that's worth a lot of money."

"But *what*?" asked Timothy.

Sarah-Jane said, "I sure wish we knew! Then Mrs. Bradley could sell whatever it is and get a lot of money. Then she wouldn't have to sell the carousel horse. And she could give it to us!"

"Maybe an expert or something could tell us what's valuable," Titus said. But he sounded tired—as if he didn't know how his idea could work.

But Sarah-Jane jumped up, full of energy. "*I* know an expert!" she cried. "See that sign down the street that says *Antiques*? That's Mr. Robinson's store. He knows my father. Let's show him our inventory lists. Maybe he can tell us what the treasure is!"

The cousins forgot all about ice-cream cones and hurried off down Main Street to Mr. Robinson's antique store.

Mr. Robinson was the kind of person who listened carefully when people talked to him. So the cousins were able to explain what they wanted him to do.

"Hmmm," he said, looking over their lists. "I'd have to see the items myself, of course, but *this* could be worth something. *That* might be valuable. Not exactly a 'gold mine' or a 'treasure,' though."

Suddenly he sat up very straight. "Tell me about this merry-go-round horse," he said quietly.

The cousins looked at one another in surprise.

34

Why did he want to know about that?

But they were good detectives, who noticed things. And they were able to describe the horse exactly—its face, its mane, its tail, its legs, its saddle, its decorations.

And the more they talked, the more Mr. Robinson listened harder and harder. "Oh, this is absolutely fabulous!" he said at last.

"You mean—*the horse* is the treasure?!" asked Sarah-Jane.

"Yes!" said Mr. Robinson. "From your description, I'd say this is a rare and beautiful carousel animal. I'm guessing it was made by one of the finest of all the carvers. I'm *also* guessing that those men are going to offer Mrs. Bradley a lot less than it's worth! We've got to warn her not to sell!"

Mr. Robinson tried to phone her. "I can't get through," he said.

"Oh, no! That's right!" cried Timothy. "Her phone is out of order!"

"Then you'd better get over there right away!" said Mr. Robinson. "I'll close up here and join you as soon as I can. Hurry!"

Titus called over his shoulder, "How much do you think the horse is worth?"

When they heard Mr. Robinson's answer, the cousins almost ran into the door.

8
DON'T SELL!

The afternoon was horribly hot. But Timothy, Titus, and Sarah-Jane ran faster than they had ever run before. And they kept on running even when their sides ached and they were out of breath.

When they *finally* turned onto Mrs. Bradley's street, they saw the men's car parked in front of her house. Then they saw the men and Mrs. Bradley and Miss Featherstone coming around the side of the house from the barn. They were all chatting in the most friendly way. One of the men got his wallet out.

Timothy took a deep breath and yelled with all his might, "DON'T SELL!"

Titus and Sarah-Jane followed his good idea. All three kids waved their arms and screamed,

"DON'T SELL! DON'T SELL!"

The cousins ran up to the yard and collapsed on the grass. Mrs. Bradley looked confused and said, "But this nice young man has just offered me *five hundred dollars* for the horse. Why shouldn't I sell?"

"Because . . ." gasped Sarah-Jane. "Mr. Robinson . . . says . . . the horse . . . might be worth . . . twenty . . . five . . . thousand . . . dollars!"

WHO'S LYING?

It took Mrs. Bradley and Miss Featherstone a few moments to understand what was happening.

The man gave a nervous little laugh. "You're not going to believe a *kid*, are you? She's just making all this up because she wants you to give her the horse."

Mrs. Bradley looked hard at the man and said, "How did *you* know I promised her that?"

"Because they were *spying* on us!" burst out Titus. "They got interested in the carousel in the library. And they eavesdropped on us. And then they followed us!"

Sarah-Jane had never seen her friend Miss Featherstone get angry before. But the old lady was *furious* now. Her face turned bright pink, and her eyes were shiny-angry.

She walked right up to the men and said, "It's true, isn't it? You *knew* a horse from the Fairfield carousel would be worth a small fortune. And you *coveted* that horse! You wanted to take it from the rightful owner. And you were willing to lie and cheat to get it!"

"What do you mean, '*cheat*'?" said the man, who was angry now, too. "That horse isn't worth *a penny* more than the five hundred I'm offering! I don't care what those little brats tell you!"

Miss Featherstone turned to Mrs. Bradley. "Lenora, I don't know about you, but I'd believe these children any day!"

Timothy said, "You don't even have to believe us. Because here comes Mr. Robinson from the antique store."

"Let's get out of here," one man muttered to the other. Then they jumped in their car and sped away.

When Mr. Robinson saw the horse, he kept saying, "Magnificent! Magnificent! It's everything I hoped it would be! You children did a wonderful job of describing it."

But something was bothering Sarah-Jane, and she had to ask Miss Featherstone about it.

They left the others in the barn and walked out under the shady trees.

"Miss Featherstone?" said Sarah-Jane in a small voice. "Did *I* do that?"

"Do what, Dear?"

"Covet Mrs. Bradley's horse. I mean—I know the last one of the Ten Commandments says 'you shall not covet.' And it's coveting when you really want something that belongs to someone else. And—and—I *really wanted* the carousel horse!''

Miss Featherstone knelt down and put her arms around Sarah-Jane. "Of *course* you wanted it, my dear! It's not wrong to want something so beautiful. But you understood that you might not be able to have it. And you accepted that. You wanted whatever was best for Mrs. Bradley.

"Someone who covets—as those two men did—acts as if *things* are more important than *people*. *You* don't act that way!''

Just then the others came out of the barn. Mr. Robinson said to Mrs. Bradley, "If you're sure you want to sell, I know I can find a buyer for you.''

"I'm sure,'' said Mrs. Bradley. "Selling Tom's carousel horse will help me out of these terrible money troubles. I think Tom would have liked that.'' She turned to Sarah-Jane. "I'm so sorry I couldn't give the horse to you, Honey.''

"That's all right,'' said Sarah-Jane, feeling very grown up. "I understand.''

Titus grinned at his cousins and said, "*Now* what do you guys want to do?''

Timothy said, "I want to rest up from all this

'NONdetective work'—especially if we're going to work on the barn again tomorrow.''

Mrs. Bradley laughed. "I'll be glad when we *finally* get this old barn all cleared out!''

"Oh, yes, indeed,'' agreed Miss Featherstone. "Because then we can start on the *attic*!''

The End

THE TEN COMMANDMENTS MYSTERIES

When Timothy, Titus, and Sarah-Jane, the three cousins, get together the most ordinary events turn into mysteries. So they've formed the T.C.D.C. (That's the Three Cousins Detective Club.)

And while the three cousins are solving mysteries, they're also learning about the Ten Commandments and living God's way.

You'll want to solve all ten mysteries along with Sarah-Jane, Ti, and Tim:

The Mystery of the Laughing Cat—"You shall not steal." *Someone stole rare coins. Can the cousins find the thief?*

The Mystery of the Messed-up Wedding—"You shall not commit adultery." *Can the cousins find the missing wedding ring?*

The Mystery of the Gravestone Riddle—"You shall not murder." *Can the cousins solve a 100-year-old murder case?*

The Mystery of the Carousel Horse—"You shall not covet." *Why does the stranger want an old, wooden horse?*

The Mystery of the Vanishing Present—"Remember the Sabbath day and keep it holy." *Can the cousins figure out who has Grandpa's missing birthday gift?*

The Mystery of the Silver Dolphin—"You shall not give false testimony." *Who's telling the truth—and who's lying?*

The Mystery of the Tattletale Parrot—"You shall not misuse the name of the Lord your God." *What will the beautiful green parrot say next?*

The Mystery of the Second Map—"You shall have no other gods before me." *Can the cousins discover who dropped the strange map?*

The Mystery of the Double Trouble—"Honor your father and your mother." *How could Timothy be in two places at once?*

The Mystery of the Silent Idol—"You shall not make for yourself an idol." *If the idol could speak, what would it tell the cousins?*

Available at your local Christian bookstore.

David C. Cook Publishing Co., Elgin, IL 60120

SHOELACES AND BRUSSELS SPROUTS

One little lie, but BIG trouble!

When Alex lies to her mom about losing her shoelaces, it doesn't seem like a big deal. But how do you replace special baseball laces when you don't have any money and you're not allowed to go to the store alone? A big softball game is coming up, and Alex knows the coach won't let her pitch in shoes without laces—or in cowboy boots!

Every kid gets into the predicaments that Alex does—ones that start out small and mushroom. Readers will learn from Alex's mistakes and understand that they have the same sources of help that she turns to: A God who loves them and wants to help them, and parents who understand.

Other books in the Alex Series . . .

2 *French Fry Forgiveness*—Sometimes making friends is harder than making enemies.

3 *Hot Chocolate Friendship*—Is winning first place as important to Alex as being a friend?

4 *Peanut Butter and Jelly Secrets*—Obeying her parents (even in little things) beats the awful results of disobeying.

Available at your local Christian bookstore.

David C. Cook Publishing Co.
850 N. Grove Ave.
Elgin, IL 60120

Chariot Books

If you liked this book, you'll also want to solve all the Beatitudes Mysteries along with Sarah-Jane, Titus, and Timothy:

The Mystery of the Empty School
"Blessed are the meek"
The Mystery of the Candy Box
"Blessed are the merciful"
The Mystery of the Disappearing Papers
"Blessed are the pure in heart"
The Mystery of the Secret Snowman
"Blessed are the peacemakers"
The Mystery of the Golden Pelican
"Blessed are those who mourn"
The Mystery of the Princess Doll
"Blessed are those who are persecuted"
The Mystery of the Hidden Egg
"Blessed are the poor in spirit"
The Mystery of the Clumsy Juggler
"Blessed are those who hunger and thirst for righteousness"